LUCKY IN LOVE

It was time to get into Conor's car and start back home. Grandpa would be waiting to see that everything had gone all right with my first attempt at waterskiing.

I started stuffing my gear into the car. But Conor just stood there. "Hey, Maureen . . ."

"Hey what?" I asked.

"Last night at the fireworks . . ."

"Yes?" Instantly I thought about the kiss, and I felt light-headed.

Conor said in a quiet voice, "I promised that would be the only kiss we'd ever have, remember?"

I couldn't speak, so I just nodded.

He moved closer to me and put a hand on my arm. "What if I broke that promise?"

"Oh, Conor!" I whispered as he pulled me into his arms.

Bantam Sweet Dreams romances
Ask your bookseller for the books you have missed

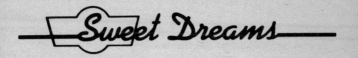

LUCKY IN LOVE

Eileen Hehl

BANTAM BOOKS
NEW YORK · TORONTO · LONDON · SYDNEY · AUCKLAND

RL 6, age 11 and up

LUCKY IN LOVE
A Bantam Book / August 1992

ISBN 0-553-29456-3

Published simultaneously in the United States and Canada

---

*Bantam Books are published by Bantam Books, a division of Bantam
Doubleday Dell Publishing Group, Inc. Its trademark, consisting of
the words "Bantam Books" and the portrayal of a rooster, is Regis-
tered in U.S. Patent and Trademark Office and in other countries.
Marca Registrada. Bantam Books, 666 Fifth Avenue, New York, New
York 10103.*

PRINTED IN THE UNITED STATES OF AMERICA

OPM   0 9 8 7 6 5 4 3 2 1

For Cathy, who helped with this book, and her tiny boy who has brought untold joy:

Michael Philip Presnick

Chapter One

I should have known there was trouble brewing.

I should have known it at the very beginning of my annual summer visit to my grandfather's when he met me at the Seabreeze bus station—but I didn't because I was too busy staring at the gorgeous guy with him.

"Hi, Maureen!" Grandpa exclaimed in his usual welcoming way, giving me a big hug. "You remember my neighbor, Conor Davis, don't you?"

"Of course," I managed to say. "Hi, Conor." I couldn't take my eyes off this boy who had suddenly—over the past winter, anyway—changed from a scrawny kid into a real hunk.

"Good to see you again, Maureen," Conor said, as my heart gave a little extra thump; even his voice was different. Deeper, and warmer. But that was nothing compared to the way he *looked.* Big, aqua-blue eyes with thick lashes and a crop of sun-bleached hair made his tanned face seem just perfect. He was tall and lean and muscular, looking great even in a pair of cutoffs and a paint-splattered rugby shirt.

Awesome! I thought. What had happened to that pesky boy who had teased me for so many summers? Not that I was interested in Conor, of course. I mean, I *was* seeing Dennis O'Brien back home in Northchester, New York, and we'd been talking about going steady after the summer.

But meanwhile, I was visiting in Seabreeze, Connecticut, for a couple of weeks. Conor Davis was shaking my hand and I didn't want him to let go.

"It's good to have you here, as always, Maureen," Grandpa said as we climbed into his beat-up old truck.

"Thanks, Grandpa," I answered. "It's great to be here."

Grandpa drove from the bus station along the Shore Road. The town of Seabreeze is right smack on Long Island Sound, so almost anywhere you go you can see expanses of salt

2

water—choppy, sunstruck, golden with light and small waves. Sailboats, cabin cruisers, fishing boats, even big liners carrying cargo bobbed on the Sound.

"How're you feeling now?" I asked Grandpa. "How's the new pacemaker working out?"

"Just fine," Grandpa said. "No problems at all."

"Really?" I asked. "Everyone at home has been worrying about you . . ."

"That's ridiculous!" Grandpa sounded impatient. "I've probably got more energy than you teenagers."

"Your grandfather has something even newer than the pacemaker this summer. . . ." Conor began, then broke off and looked at Grandpa with concern. "Is it okay to mention it, Captain Andy?" *Captain Andy* was the name most people in Seabreeze called my grandpa, because he used to be in the boating business. He'd retired about ten years ago.

Grandpa glanced over at me. "If Maureen can keep a secret, yes. Can you, young lady?"

"Of course, I can!" I said eagerly. "I'll explode if you don't tell me!"

"You can't mention this to your mother," Grandpa warned, "and you especially must not tell your Uncle Reggie."

What in the world could Grandpa be up to?

"I think Maureen can be trusted," Conor said.

Grandpa nodded, then made a left turn at a sign that said Kelley's Marina instead of following Shore Road to his house. I was getting more curious by the minute!

We drove along a bumpy dirt road until we were almost at the water's edge. Kelley's was a boat yard and marina, with a maze of wooden docks where all sorts of boats were kept in the small harbor. The boat yard itself was full of many boats in dry dock, and Grandpa's truck stopped near one of them. I noticed that he was fidgeting almost nervously, which was unlike him. I guessed that there was something here that was very important to him. But what?

"See that Chris-Craft up there?" Grandpa asked, pointing at a big wreck of a boat.

I looked up. The boat he pointed to was a wretched mass of weathered, splintered wood that was barely held together by a few rusty nails. It was the most pitiful sight I'd ever seen.

"That's my new boat," Grandpa said proudly.

This awful wreck was the vital new item in Grandpa's life? Oh *no*!

"What do you mean?" I gasped. "You *bought* that boat, Grandpa?"

"I sure did." He grinned from ear to ear. "I'm going to restore her, and I'm calling her the *Lucky Lindie.* She's going to be an exquisite classic when we're finished with her."

Exquisite? That? I couldn't speak, so I got out of the truck and circled around the old hulk. I saw big holes in the hull, varnish peeling everywhere, and barnacles encrusting the bottom. But I knew I had to be very careful not to hurt Grandpa's feelings.

"The *Lucky Lindie,*" I repeated as he and Conor joined me. "You named her after Grandma Linda." My grandmother had died three years ago, and Grandpa had been living alone since then.

"I sure did. Young Conor here is helping me with the restoration. He's my official apprentice and helper."

"Oh, that's right," I said, hoping to change the subject. "You come from a family of shipbuilders, don't you, Conor?"

"I do." Conor spoke with fierce New England pride. It was strange to have him looking down at me. How had he gotten so *tall,* for heaven's sake?

"Pretty special boat, isn't she?" Grandpa was obviously eager to hear my verdict. "She's a classic Chris-Craft from the fifties, a cabin cruiser you can sleep on. They don't make wooden boats like this anymore, you know."

"Really?" I said faintly.

"That's right," Grandpa said. "Everybody's buying those newfangled fiberglass things these days. Well, Maureen, what do you think?"

I stood there in the shade of a big old maple, desperately trying to find the right words. At last I said, "I think if anyone in the world can restore her, it's you guys. I think she's going to be beautiful." As the words emerged, I was surprised to realize that I meant it. "And she's truly *lucky* to have two such skilled craftsmen working on her."

"You got that right," Conor said with a big grin. One thing hadn't changed about Conor—he'd always had a healthy ego when it came to his skills with boats.

I grinned, too, and turned to Grandpa. "So I guess I think—it's wonderful." I pretended to hold up a champagne glass. "Here's to the *Lucky Lindie!*"

Grandpa gave me a hug, and Conor reached out and patted me on the back. At his touch, my pulse began to race double time.

"You're okay, Maureen," he said in his old teasing manner, "even if you *are* a New York landlubber."

When we were younger, Conor used to try to annoy me any way he could. Now I saw a quick flash of that mischievous boy in his handsome face—but I also saw something else. I could tell that Conor was as surprised at how much I'd changed over the past year as I was at the changes in him. Maybe he was noticing that my braces had finally been removed, and that my hair was thick and full instead of straggly. And my tight jeans and snug-fitting T-shirt revealed that my figure wasn't bad at all. Maureen Butler was a *girl*. Evidently he'd never noticed that before, or else he hadn't cared until now.

"I hope you'll let me help with the boat, too, Grandpa," I said quickly. "I've never worked on anything like this, but . . ."

"Of course, honey, and you can learn." Grandpa sounded delighted. "Consider yourself an official member of the *Lindie* crew."

I felt happy, and I knew at that point that I was going to have a *very* interesting summer.

Chapter Two

"Are you positive you don't want to back out of this project?" Grandpa asked me about an hour later. The sun was setting and we were still up on the deck of the *Lucky Lindie.*

"Not a chance!" I peeled off a flake of ancient paint. "I can't wait to start cleaning— or whatever it is we do first."

She was a good-size boat, I had to admit. The cabin was roomy enough for a small kitchen with a table, and the table could convert to beds when you needed to sleep.

"Wow, there's even a bathroom in here!" I cried when I opened a little door toward the front of the cabin.

"That's called the head," Conor corrected me. "Not the bathroom."

"And that's the bow section, not the front, Maureen." Grandpa gave a little chuckle. "Might as well start teaching you the correct names for nautical things."

"Might as well," I said cheerfully. I breathed in the tangy seaside air. "Is it just me, or does this boat yard atmosphere make everybody ravenously hungry? Are we having supper at the Seabreeze Diner, Grandpa?" I asked. We had always gone to the diner the first night I was in town, even when Grandma had been alive.

"Of course. Would you like to join us for dinner, Conor?" Grandpa asked.

"Thanks, Captain Andy, but I've got to be getting home." Conor grinned. "You know, my mother always makes a big batch of baked beans on Saturdays, and all the family gathers for that. I might come by your place later this evening," Conor said. "Maybe Maureen would like to take a walk by the water . . . there are going to be some fireworks tonight."

"Fireworks?" I repeated in surprise, not only because I'd forgotten it was the Fourth of July, but because I was amazed that Conor was actually inviting me to go out with him.

"Thanks but I can't," I said. "I always spend my first night here with Grandpa."

Conor was silent for a moment, gazing at

me in a thoughtful way, as if trying to assess what was in my mind. Maybe he wasn't used to girls saying no to him.

"Okay," he finally said with a shrug.

We all climbed down from the boat, scrambling over the rough wooden planks.

"I'll have to buy a good strong ladder," Grandpa mumbled, pulling a notepad out of his pocket and making several scribbled notes.

"Cap'n Andy and his famous notebook," Conor said, chuckling.

We paused under a giant oak tree, and shafts of sunlight through the leaves dappled Conor's blond hair. His nose was nice and straight, and I couldn't help noticing that his eyes were the color of the water in the harbor.

"See you," Conor said casually while I was still staring at him, then turned and disappeared among all the dry-docked boats. I was left feeling sort of disappointed and empty. I'd thought he would ride back home with us. Why hadn't I said yes to his fireworks invitation? Grandpa probably wouldn't have minded. . . .

I shook my head to clear away the cobwebs. *Don't be silly*, I told myself. *You're not one bit interested in Conor Davis. He's just a friend.* In the past, he hadn't even been that.

11

He'd been a nuisance who delighted in tormenting me. Just last summer he'd crashed his bike into mine on Shore Road. Of course he said it wasn't deliberate, but we'd both been angry and started calling each other names.

Funny, remembering that incident now made it feel so long ago. It wasn't just because Conor had grown tall and filled out. He seemed to have matured in other ways, too, and I liked that.

But, as I said, I wasn't looking for a boyfriend. Dennis O'Brien was waiting for me back home in New York. Dennis was a great guy—good looking and brainy. Like me, he planned to go to a top college for a business degree. So there was no possible reason to get a crush—even a very small one—on Conor Davis. None at all.

Every July when I visited Grandpa, we had our same sacred tradition. We always ate meatballs, spaghetti, and crusty garlic bread at the diner on my first evening. And that's exactly what we did that night.

"Remember how your grandmother used to love garlic bread?" Grandpa asked me after we'd given our order to the waitress.

My eyes filled with sudden stinging tears, and I nodded.

Grandpa put a hand out to cover mine on the table. "It still hurts to talk about Grandma Linda, doesn't it?"

"Yes," I murmured.

He said quietly, "That was one lady who wouldn't want us to sit around crying for her, you know."

"I do know, but it's hard. I miss her a lot, Grandpa."

"Of course, and so do I. But your grandma would want us to think fondly of her, and then go on with our lives *without* tears."

I nodded again.

"I like to think of this new boat project as one way of my going on with my life, Maureen," Grandpa said. "It gives me a purpose, something to get excited about, something to make me want to get out of bed each morning."

"That sounds terrific," I answered. "But . . ."

"But what?"

"Well, this business about keeping the boat a secret from the family. I'm not so sure about that."

"I see." Grandpa sat back in the diner booth, frowning a little. He was a nice-looking man, sort of round and well padded but not really fat. His head was mostly bald except for a ring of curly white hair, and he wore brown-framed glasses that circled his kind, intelligent eyes. I noticed that he had a good tan; evidently he'd been getting lots of sun at the boat yard.

"I guess I really didn't explain why I want to keep quiet about the boat," Grandpa said at last. "As you know, I had that pacemaker put in during the winter. I feel wonderful, like a new man. But your mother, and your uncle Reggie—"

"Are always worrying about you," I finished for him.

"It's worse than that. Your uncle wants to stick me away in some kind of a retirement home, one of those places where there would be nurses to keep an eye on me day and night."

"Oh, Grandpa, that sounds awful!"

"It sure does!" Grandpa was indignant. "But try to tell Reginald that. He keeps urging me to sell my little house and move to New York State to be near him and your folks."

"That kind of decision should be up to you!" I exclaimed.

"Yes, it should. I'm perfectly healthy now, and my doctor says I should go on the way I've been."

"But Grandpa," I said, "does your doctor know about this boat project?"

He grinned widely. "Heck, yes! Doc Barnett has a yacht in Kelley's Marina himself. In fact he was the one who told me about the *Lindie* when she came in and was put up for sale. But that still won't satisfy your uncle Reggie. It seems easier to keep the *Lucky Lindie* a secret for now. I don't want to get into big arguments with my son and daughter." Grandpa smiled at the waitress as she brought us our garlic bread.

I thought about Uncle Reggie; everyone knew he never took no for an answer. He was an attorney who always won every case. If he was a meddler, my mother was a serious worrier. They'd both have a fit if they suspected Grandpa was doing hard physical labor after getting the pacemaker.

So at that moment I made my decision, for better or worse. I would keep Grandpa's secret as long as he truly was in good health. And just as soon as possible and as quietly as possible, I planned to check with this Dr. Barnett to be sure.

"Okay, Grandpa," I said. "My lips are sealed." I made a zipper motion across my mouth, and he grinned widely.

"Everything will be fine, you'll see," Grandpa said.

I certainly hope so, Captain Andy, I thought.

When we finally reached Grandpa's house, we heard the telephone ringing. Grandpa hurried to answer it while I lingered outside, savoring my feelings of nostalgia.

I loved this house on Lilac Lane. It was only half a block from the Sound, so if you looked over the hedges you could see waves dancing out beyond the breakwater. Grandma had been a terrific gardener, and the whole yard was always filled with seasonal flowers: lilacs, tulips, and daffodils in the spring, and hollyhocks, roses, and masses of daylilies in summer.

For the past couple of summers when I came to Connecticut, Grandpa obviously hadn't been bothering much with the flowers. But now I was surprised to see that the garden looked fabulous. There wasn't a weed to be seen! How had Grandpa had time for all this, I wondered, and time to plan his new boat project as well?

But before I had time to think about it further, Grandpa called me. "Telephone, Maureen. Your mom."

I went inside, bracing myself for my mother's inquisition.

"Hi, Mom."

"Hi, dear. Have a good trip?"

"Yes, it was great."

"How does your grandpa look? Is he healthy?"

"He sure is! He's got a great tan, and—"

16

"But does he seem tired?"

"No, not at all. He—"

"Maureen, listen carefully to me. Your uncle and I are trying to get a handle on how Grandpa *really* is. He's always saying everything's fine, but . . ."

"Things really *are* fine, Mom." I winked at Grandpa, who was standing nearby with a big smile, shamelessly eavesdropping.

"Maureen," Mom continued, "is the house filthy? Is the refrigerator empty? Is the garden a mess?"

I looked around the room. "Honestly, there's not a speck of dust anywhere, Mom. The housekeeping is"—I tried to find just the right word—"impeccable."

"Don't be silly," she said impatiently. "We all know Grandpa hates to clean house."

"I'm telling the simple truth. The house looks terrific. And the garden—I just strolled through it, and it looked as if Grandma Linda never left."

The silence was deafening. My mother knew I wasn't a liar, so she had to believe me.

"I don't understand," Mom said finally.

"Me neither," I agreed amiably.

"Well, Maureen, keep your eyes open, will you? I'm terribly concerned about Grandpa. Make sure he doesn't overdo it, honey. Make

sure he eats right, and please report anything to us that you think we should know."

At those words, I felt distinctly uncomfort-
able. Did that include the boat? Well, I was
committed to silence, for better or worse. Besides, the boat was *not* something I thought
she should know about, so I guessed it was
okay.

"Maybe he's got a cleaning woman coming
in," my mother mused aloud. "Snoop around,
will you, dear?"

"I definitely will, Mom," I said. That was
true, too. I intended to talk to Dr. Barnett
as soon as possible. As to the immaculate
condition of the house and garden, I was
pretty curious, too.

Chapter Three

I had another big surprise later as I took out Scrabble for our traditional "first-night game." "How do you feel about playing with three?" Grandpa asked in an offhand way as he set out the letter tiles.

"Three what?" I asked.

"Three people." He cleared his throat. "There's a friend I'd like you to meet, if you agree."

I stared at my grandfather. A friend? This was something new! Usually nothing—and no one—was allowed to violate our first night together.

"Sure," I finally said. "I'd like to meet your friend."

Grandpa made a quick phone call, then turned back to me. "She'll be right over."

"She?" I said surprised. *So it is a female friend,* I thought.

He blushed a little bit. "Her name is Claire MacPhearson—she's a widow. Most of the young folks in Seabreeze call her Mrs. Mac."

I didn't have time to ask any questions, because just then I heard a brisk knock on the back door.

"She lives only two houses away," Grandpa told me, smiling like a little kid as he went to open the door.

A moment later, a tiny lady with pure white hair came bouncing in, and I do mean *bouncing;* she had a genuine spring in her step.

"Hi, Maureen," she said. "I'm Claire Mac."

We shook hands. "Glad to meet you," I mumbled.

"The pleasure is mine," she said. "I've been hearing so much about this super special granddaughter of Andy's. He said you're a wonderful Scrabble player."

Grandpa seemed eager for us to like each other, so, of course, I did my best to be cordial. "I—I think it's great that Grandpa has a new friend," I stammered. "Especially someone who lives so close by . . ."

"Claire's a gourmet cook," Grandpa said

proudly. "She keeps me well fed, with properly balanced meals. And she loves to garden."

"Oh!" Light dawned in my brain. "The garden . . . was it you, Mrs. Mac, who made it so beautiful this summer?"

Mrs. Mac nodded modestly.

"Yes, and the foolish woman insists on coming in here to clean the house, too," Grandpa said.

"It looks spotless," I admitted. "I was amazed at how Grandpa managed to dust every single item in the parlor as well as have the kitchen floor sparkling!"

All three of us laughed, knowing how Grandpa detested housework. The ice was broken at that moment. Right then, I decided that I liked Mrs. Mac. She was very attractive, I thought. There was something grandmotherly about her small face and white hair, but she was pretty trendy, too, with her stylish blue silk scarf and powder-blue workout clothes.

Maybe there was more to Grandpa's "getting on" with his life than I had suspected. Grandpa had a girlfriend! Lady-friend? Friend-friend?

What would Uncle Reggie and my mother have to say about *that*?

*   *   *

We were almost finished with the first Scrabble game when there was another knock on the door.

"This sure is a busy place tonight," I said, jumping up. I opened the back door in the kitchen and did a double take.

Conor Davis stood there, grinning and looking fabulous in a bright yellow T-shirt that read Save the Whales and a pair of khaki pants. Quite a change from the grungy, faded clothes he'd been wearing earlier that day.

"Hi, Maureen," he said cheerfully. "Came to see if you'd changed your mind. The fireworks are about to start down on the beach."

"Why don't you go, dear?" Mrs. Mac called out. "I'll keep your grandfather company."

"I don't mind if you go out, Maureen," Grandpa echoed. "The fireworks are pretty spectacular on the Fourth."

Just then the whoosh of a rocket sounded from the direction of the beach, and I didn't have to think it over for long.

"Okay," I said, feeling a rush of excitement. "I'll go grab my windbreaker."

"Take a heavy sweater," Grandpa advised as I rummaged around in my suitcase. "Gets cold out there at night."

So I threw my thickest pullover around my shoulders, ran a comb through my hair, and dabbed some light lip gloss on my lips.

Perfume? I pondered that for half a second, then decided against it. This was not a real date. It was just a last-minute outing with Grandpa's apprentice/helper.

"See you later, Grandpa, and nice to meet you, Mrs. Mac," I said, waving as Conor and I went out the door.

The night might turn chilly later, but it still felt like balmy, moist July. The sounds of crickets and birds were in the air. A sliver of a new moon hung high in the night sky. We walked side by side, not speaking.

"This was a great idea," I finally said to break the silence. "I'm glad you asked me again."

"Um-hmm," he said.

I started to chuckle. "Have you turned into one of those strong, silent types, like those grim New England seafaring men who never waste a word?"

"Maybe." I could see his grinning face in what moonlight there was.

"We don't have much in common, then," I said merrily. "I'm the talkative type who's always shooting off her mouth, especially at school."

"I know exactly what kind of girl you are," Conor said. "You get all *A*'s, and I bet you're on the Student Council."

"Yes," I said, surprised that he knew so much about me.

"You've got all your college applications made out already," he continued.

"Well, yes . . ."

"And you figure you'll need at least an MBA in order to get somewhere in life."

"How do you *know* all that?" I demanded.

"Because." He smiled down at me as we walked. "I know a lot of girls just like you. The intellectual type, you might say."

"Oh, really?" I loved to read, and I actually enjoyed studying, but I had never thought of myself as "intellectual," and it sounded strange to hear Conor describing me that way.

"Yep." He kept strolling along, his head down and his eyes on the path in front of us. "The kind of girl I *never* get involved with."

"Why?" I asked, intrigued.

"Because, as you said, we have nothing in common." He glanced over at me with a frown. "I don't plan to go to college, I don't need an MBA, and I don't like girls who think I do."

"But . . ."

"Nothing in common," Conor said firmly, walking faster. His legs were so long that I had to scramble just to keep up.

"Even if you're right," I said, "and maybe

24

you are, then why did you ask me to go to the fireworks with you tonight?"

"Why?" Conor stopped beside the stone pillars at the entrance to the beach. I stopped, too, and looked up at him. *Way* up, because he was a full head taller than me. "I figured we ought to try being friends," he said slowly. "After all, we'll be working together on the *Lucky Lindie* for a few weeks."

I nodded.

"Might as well not harbor any grudges from the old days."

I chuckled. "You mean, back when you used to splash me at the beach till I nearly drowned? And crash into my bike? And put snakes in my beach bag?"

"The snake thing wasn't me!" he protested. "That was Jason Platt. I'd never scare a girl with snakes!"

"I see," I said, smiling. "Glad to hear that, anyway."

"I'm a decent kind of guy, maybe a little old-fashioned," Conor said. "Maybe even kind of square. I just want you to know that about me."

"Okay," I said.

"Also, I never date college type girls, and I have no intentions of going to college myself, *ever*," he added.

"But I never said . . ." I began.

25

"Sooner or later every girl starts to lecture me about it. I'm going to be a shipbuilder, just like my grandfather, my father, my brothers, and my uncles. That's all I want to do, and you don't need a college education for that."

"Aye, aye, sir." I saluted with exaggeration. "I get the message loud and clear. Over and out!"

"Wise guy," Conor said, grinning, and reaching out to take my hand. "No wonder—all New Yorkers are wise guys. Come on. Let's get to the beach before the fireworks are all over."

Purple rockets! Silvery explosions! Pink-and-blue expanding spheres of fire! Loud pops that made everyone jump and then clap with delight!

Enchanted, I sat on the beach gazing upward, and Conor sat beside me, still holding my hand. I didn't know what to make of that; it didn't make any sense at all after that whole speech about being friends and about him never dating girls who planned to go to college.

Finally I decided that he was probably trying to make some other girl jealous. We were surrounded by a large crowd, mostly kids from the local high school where Conor went.

Every minute or so, someone would say hi to him and stare at me, wondering who I was.

"Here comes the finale," Conor whispered, moving closer to me. His lips so near to my ear made me shiver for a moment. It was odd, because being with Dennis had never made me shiver.

One last spectacular display lit up the entire sky, sparkling, popping, and exploding with all the colors of the rainbow. It was so beautiful, it took my breath away. Just as the finale ended, Conor's arm encircled my shoulder and I leaned against him. Before I had a chance to realize what was happening, he gently kissed my cheek, just an inch from my mouth.

My heart pounded. "Why'd you do that?" I asked.

He grinned. "It's an old Connecticut custom—like mistletoe."

"Huh?"

"You're supposed to kiss somebody during the fireworks finale on the Fourth of July," he said.

"I never heard of that tradition." I stared at him suspiciously.

"You heard of it now," Conor responded, still grinning. "Anyway, it was also my way of saying I'm sorry I crashed into your bike last year."

I was too astonished to answer. My cheek felt warm, almost burning hot, where his lips had touched.

He stood up and brushed the sand off the back of his pants. "Don't worry, Maureen. That'll be the only kiss. I promise."

I stood up, too, still staring at him.

"I mean it," he said. "There's no sense in starting anything, right?"

"Absolutely not," I managed to say, a little disappointed.

We walked home in comfortable silence. Conor didn't hold my hand. At the door of Grandpa's house he kept his distance, smiling pleasantly.

"Thanks for taking me to the fireworks," I said. "I really enjoyed it."

"Me, too. I'm glad we're friends." Conor's eyes were a deep, dusky blue under the porch light. "G'night."

He was already loping across the lawn when I answered, "Goodnight." I watched him until he disappeared into the shadows. Then I put my fingers up to touch my cheek where he had kissed me. I couldn't help but wonder what the rest of the summer might bring.

Chapter Four

"Guess what?" Grandpa said the next day as we ate breakfast. "Today's our first official day of boat renovation!"

"Oh, really?" I felt excited already. "What should I wear, Grandpa? Something old, I guess?"

He laughed. "Yes, real old duds. Everything we do will be messy and probably even destructive to your clothes. Did you bring anything you don't care about?"

"No," I answered. As usual, I had packed only my best and newest summer clothes.

"Take a look in the big trunk in the cellar," Grandpa suggested. "Your grandma stashed away a bunch of old jeans and shirts down there. She couldn't bear to throw anything away."

As soon as we'd finished eating I went to the basement. Grandma's "rag box" was a treasure trove of ancient clothes. Right away I found several old pairs of jeans. One had a ripped knee and the other was missing a button at the waist, but I didn't care. They were fine for our nautical work.

Grandpa was ready to go before I'd changed into the jeans and a faded old shirt. But when I went out to the truck, I found him annoyed, poking under its hood.

"Darned shifting mechanism," he was mumbling. "Never a minute's peace with this old rattletrap."

"What's wrong with it?" I asked, watching to see what he was fixing.

"The linkage comes undone sometimes. It's easy to fix but it can be a nuisance. . . ." He deftly connected several strange pieces of metal and before long the old pickup truck was back in business.

"I can't imagine how you know how to do all that, Grandpa," I said, shaking my head.

"Just comes from years of experience," Grandpa said with a grin. "But you'll have to learn to fix that shifting thing, too, Maureen, if you ever plan to drive the truck this summer."

"Me? No way! I'm the least mechanical person. I'm the family bookworm, remember?"

"Don't sell yourself short, Maureen. Sometimes situations arise where you have to know such things."

He showed me again what he'd done. Though I tried to memorize it, my brain told me I might be a bookworm and an honor student, but definitely *not* a girl who could monkey with a motor.

"I'll try to remember, Grandpa," I told him, thinking that I'd probably never need to drive the truck, anyway. Everything I wanted in the town of Seabreeze was within walking distance—the beach, the library, even the shopping center.

Kelley's Marina, however, was a few miles away. We drove over there immediately.

Mr. Kelley came out to welcome us. "It's a glorious day, Cap'n Andy," he said. "Great day for working on your boat."

"Sure is," Grandpa said. "Ken Kelley, this is my granddaughter, Maureen Butler, who came all the way from New York to help."

Mr. Kelley and I shook hands. He was a tall man, with a broad, friendly face.

"That's going to be the finest wooden boat afloat one day," Mr. Kelley told me, pointing to the *Lindie*. "I'm here to tell you I'll help your granddad in any way I can."

"That's great," I answered. But when I looked up at the *Lucky Lindie*, she looked every bit as pitiful as she had yesterday. Maybe even worse. *Sometimes you've just got to have faith*, I figured. *Hang in there and give it a shot.*

Then a man walked over to the boat with his arms full of tools.

"Hi there. I'm Dr. Barnett," he said, looking at me. "Came to give you a hand!" He looked less like an eminent cardiologist than like somebody's deckhand. He was thin and gray haired and wore ancient clothes.

"Nice to meet you," I said.

"Need me to climb into the bilge and poke around?" he asked cheerfully.

"You're hired," Grandpa exclaimed.

"Great!" Dr. Barnett said. "Let's get started."

Just as we were all starting to climb up on the platform that held the boat, Conor came driving into the boat yard in an old Ford. My stomach jumped at the sight of him as I remembered his soft kiss last night.

Just friends, I reminded myself. *Friends. Remember that, Maureen.* But why did he have to look so great this morning, even in those old paint-splattered cutoffs?

"Morning, all," Conor said, strutting over

to the *Lindie* as if he owned it. "Mornin',
Maureen."

"Hi," I said casually.

"I guess we ought to divide up the first
day's projects," Grandpa said with great enthusiasm. "Dr. B., you mentioned going into
the bilge to find bad planks, so that's your
assignment."

"Aye, aye, Cap'n." The doctor looked delighted.

Grandpa continued, "Conor, how about
getting started on sanding and scraping the
hull?"

"Fine."

"And Ken, you told me the other day you
have a power wash we can use?"

"Right," Mr. Kelley said. "I'll go get it."

"Great. And let's see now. Maureen . . ."

My heart sank. What if Grandpa couldn't
find a job for the "landlubber"? I began to
feel like a real loser who didn't have a useful
skill in the world.

"What if I work on these rusted doodads?"
I asked suddenly, pointing to some oddly
shaped things I'd been looking at.

"Good idea!" Grandpa said. "They're all
chrome and brass, and they need to be removed and polished. I'll just start checking
the ribs with Dr. B. . . ." He loped off toward
his job.

"Maureen, these things are not called doo-dads," Conor said to me condescendingly. "They each have a name, like cleats, scuppers, gas cap . . ." His patronizing tone set me on edge.

"Listen, Conor," I snapped, standing up very straight. "I realize I don't know a thing about boats. And you, of course, know everything, because your ancestors probably built the *Mayflower,* at the very least!"

"I'd hardly say that—" he began.

"Give me a break, okay? Don't treat me like I'm some airhead, because I'm not!"

His eyebrows shot up in surprise. "Fair enough," he said, raising his hands in surrender. "Sorry."

"Thank you," I retorted with dignity. "Now. I'm dying to get started and eager to learn, but from a teacher who *doesn't* patronize me."

"Okay, okay, okay!" Conor said. His face was slightly flushed, as if he were ashamed of himself. "Here are some of the tools you'll need." Politely and patiently, Conor gave me a crash course on removing the chrome and brass items with a screwdriver and a pair of pliers. It was all brand-new to me, and I found it interesting. By the time Conor went off to start sanding the hull, I was hard at work.

A few hours later, Dr. Barnett said to me, "Hey, you're doing great, Maureen. With all those pieces out of the way, the work'll go smoother as we strip each section of wood."

"Thanks," I said. Then I lowered my voice. "Dr. Barnett, I need to talk to you privately. Is my grandpa around?"

"No. He just went over to Mr. Kelley's office. What's the problem?"

"Well, it's about Grandpa's health . . ." I stopped, unsure of what I should ask. "My mother worries about him a lot, you see. So does my uncle Reggie, and so do I. I just want to be sure it's safe for Grandpa to be doing all this hard work on the boat." I shaded my eyes from the noonday sun and looked up at the doctor. "*Is* it safe?"

"Absolutely. Your grandfather is in excellent shape. That pacemaker will keep him going for a long, long time."

I sighed with relief. "That's what he's been telling me, but I had to be absolutely certain. You see, he's keeping all of this work on the *Lucky Lindie* a secret from the rest of the family."

"It's his right." Dr. Barnett grinned and put a hand on my shoulder. "Don't worry, Maureen. I give my complete sanction to your grandpa's project."

"Thanks, Dr. B.," I said simply.

"Well, what's going on here? A high-level conference?" Grandpa returned just then from the boat yard office, carrying ice cold cans of soda for everyone.

Sitting up on deck, I took a break and sipped at my soda while Dr. B. conferred with Grandpa about what they had found in the boat's hull—a few planks had to be replaced, but not really anything too terrible. Mr. Kelley was setting up the power-wash machine down below, connecting extension cords so he could plug it in. Conor was sanding the part of the boat that would be above water when she set sail. Sanding the very bottom of the hull would be one of the last jobs done.

I looked down at Conor's thatch of blond hair as he worked doggedly with the power sander. Maybe I should consider staying all summer, I thought. After all, Grandpa would be needing all the help he could get. . . .

I realized I was still staring at Conor. Good thing he couldn't see me! Then he stopped working and stretched his long, muscular legs and arms.

Yes, maybe I *would* stay all summer. I was sure Mom and Dad wouldn't mind. What was there at home, anyway? Just Dennis and that SAT prep course we'd planned to take together.

Oh, Maureen, you used to be so practical and now you're becoming a romantic, I chided myself.

But I didn't care. I was having fun, more fun than I'd had in years. I began to hum an old Beatles song as I went back to my job of unscrewing the cleats.

Around one o'clock, Mrs. Mac arrived with a giant picnic basket. "Sandwiches, fresh fruit, milk," she called out as if she were a street vendor, setting up a small card table under the maple trees. "Come and get it! And for dessert, my special sinful, three-layer, double chocolate cake!"

"Which is totally against doctor's orders," the cardiologist said immediately with a twinkle in his eye. "Except for me, that is."

I went to the ladies' rest room over in the main building of the marina to give my hands a good washing; I was covered with rust and flakes of paint from head to toe. I washed my face, too, and ran a comb through my long brown hair. As I came out of the ladies' room, Conor caught up with me.

"How's it going?" he asked, falling into step beside me and heading back across the yard.

"Good," I said. "I think. I got all the *cleats*

off, and the *scuppers,* and next is the fuel filler plate . . ."

He chuckled. "You learn pretty fast, especially for an airhead!"

"I'll airhead you!" I hollered, pretending to swat him, though I knew he was teasing. "You know something, Conor?" I said. "You're really not all that different from the mean little kid who used to ruin my summers."

"Oh, yes I am," he said quietly with a smile.

I shivered slightly, because I could have sworn Conor was looking at me the way a guy looks at a girl he finds attractive. And that was ridiculous, because I was dressed in the world's worst clothes from the rag bin!

"If you're so different, why don't you stop annoying me then?" I said lightly, falling into his playful mood.

He laughed. "Because it's such a blast teasing a New York honor student. Hey, how would you like to go waterskiing after supper?"

Surprised, I blinked. "You have a boat?"

"My brother does. And I'm a good, safe boater, certified by the Power Squadron, believe it or not."

"I believe you." I gazed into his blue eyes. "I've always wanted to try waterskiing . . ."

"Then say yes."

"*Yes.* I'd love to go."

"Good. Check with your grandfather, and if it's okay, I'll pick you up around six."

Another date with Conor, I thought, hurrying over to help Mrs. Mac set out the food from her picnic basket.

Another invitation from the boy who says we're just friends, and we have nothing in common. Things were getting more interesting by the minute!

Chapter Five

Early that evening when we were getting ready for dinner, I heard Grandpa on the phone.

"No, Reginald," Grandpa was saying, "I don't care how many swimming pools the Sunset Home has for heart patients. I live right on the Sound, remember?"

Poor Grandpa, I thought. He was so happy with all these new friends and activities, and now he had to deal with Uncle Reggie, who could be a regular steamroller when he pursued something.

"No, Reggie. Absolutely not. I don't *want* to meet that new doctor you found—"

Grandpa was interrupted, then he spoke

again. "I'm satisfied with *my* cardiologist, thank you very much, and I'm staying with *him*. I'm also staying right here in Connecticut."

There was a long silence while Grandpa listened.

"Fine," he said at last. "Good-bye, then." Grandpa called to me. "Maureen? Your uncle wants to talk to you." He made a face like that of a naughty little boy as he handed me the phone. I almost burst out laughing.

"Maureen!" Uncle Reggie's voice sounded clipped and angry.

"Yes, sir?" I said.

"Your mother tells me you're staying in Connecticut for a couple of weeks."

"Yes, Uncle Reggie, and maybe even longer."

Grandpa looked pleased to hear that.

"Oh, really? Why is that?" my uncle asked.

"Well . . ." I knew I had to be careful. I couldn't say that Grandpa seemed to need me, because that would sound as if he were sick and required constant attention. And I certainly couldn't say I was having the time of my life working on a classic Chris-Craft boat that happened to belong to my grandfather!

"It's fun to be away from home for a change," I said truthfully. "And I do enjoy Grandpa's company."

"Huh!" Uncle Reggie sounded skeptical. "You're keeping an eye on the old man, to see if he's really as healthy as he claims?"

I felt a rush of anger at my uncle for calling Grandpa "the old man," but I didn't give in to it at first. "Yes. Mom told me to."

"Well, make sure you report everything to us, Maureen. Do you understand?"

"Uncle Reggie, I don't think that's necessary. I—"

"We're not asking you to *think*, young lady. Just give us the facts and we'll decide what ought to be done."

"You're being awfully unfair," I blurted out. "Grandpa is more than capable of running his own life!"

"We'll see about that." Uncle Reggie gave a big, exaggerated sigh of frustration. "I'll be out there to see for myself as soon as I can get away."

"You don't need to do that!" I said quickly. "We're just fine, really."

"I'll see you *soon*, Maureen," he repeated firmly.

"Fine," I said, forcing a pleasant tone. "We'll be sure to leave the porch light on for you."

Uncle Reggie said good-bye and hung up. Grandpa had been listening to my end of the conversation, trying not to laugh out loud.

"Your son is turning into a monster," I told him, giggling.

"He always *was* a monster!" Grandpa joked. "Ever since he became an attorney, he's been a Legal Monster!"

We laughed throughout our whole meal, which was take-out Chinese food. But when we broke open our fortune cookies, Grandpa made a serious face.

He said, "Uh-oh. Listen to my fortune. 'Beware of a man who will arrive unexpectedly.' "

"What a coincidence!" I said. "But it can't mean Uncle Reggie, because we're expecting him, so it's okay."

"What does your fortune say?" Grandpa asked me.

I opened it with mixed feelings. I didn't really believe in this stuff, and yet . . .

I stared at the small printed message that popped out of my cookie and actually felt a tiny shock wave go through me. My fortune said: Love blossoms in an unexpected place . . . pay heed to a man of the sea.

When I read it aloud, Grandpa scratched his head and smiled mysteriously. "A man of the sea? Sounds like Conor, if you ask me."

"No way!" I said quickly. I could feel the blood rushing to my face as I tossed the fortune away. "Conor and me? That would be ridiculous."

44

"I've known Conor all his life, and he's a fine young man," Grandpa said quietly, never taking his eyes from my face.

"I'm sure he is, but . . ."

"But what?"

"Oh, Grandpa, we have absolutely nothing in common."

"Who says so?" Grandpa challenged.

"I did. He did. We both did! Besides, he doesn't go for girls like me," I told him. "He said that himself. So there's not a chance."

"That's strange." Grandpa sat back with an amused smile. "I thought maybe Conor had something to do with your thinking of staying longer. I also thought I heard you say you were going out waterskiing with a certain someone this evening. What was his name again?"

"Conor, but don't get any wrong ideas." I picked up the plates and cleared the table rapidly. "We're just friends, Grandpa, nothing more."

"If you say so," Grandpa said amiably. "Who believes what a fortune cookie predicts, anyway?"

Riding in an open speedboat brought a constant spray of salt water, but it felt heavenly. We'd had a long, hot day working in the boat yard and now at last Conor and I were whizzing across Long Island Sound in a boat named *Lazy Bones*, feeling cool and refreshed.

In front of us, the wide expanse of the Sound gleamed bluish silver, choppy with small waves. The coastline sped by, and trees, homes, and marinas looked far away and miniature.

"It's so beautiful," I shouted over the roar of the powerful engine.

"Glad you're enjoying it." Conor never took his eyes off the waterway in front of him. As he had said, he was a careful boater.

Conor's friend Jason Platt, who had put the snake in my beach bag years ago, and his girlfriend, Kristina, were with us. They sat in the stern, quite obviously looking me over.

"Conor said you're going to be a senior in the fall, like us," Kristina had said when we were first introduced. "Then you're going to college?"

"Yes," I answered. "Maybe Columbia University, if they accept me, or Long Island University."

"Not me!" Kristina, blond, tall, and heavily made up, looked down at her long fingernails. "I've been in vocational school for three years, learning beauty."

"As in beauty parlor? That's great," I said politely.

"College isn't for everybody," Jason said cheerfully. "Right, Conor?"

"Right." That ended the discussion, which was fine with me. I didn't feel like debating.

When we were way out in deep water, Conor slowed the boat and Jason dug out the skis, life belts, and towrope. I began to get a little nervous. The water looked so dark and mysterious . . .

"Who's first?" Jason asked. "Maureen?"

I shook my head. "No. I've never done it before, so I want to watch first."

Jason jumped in, disappeared for a moment, and came up wet and jubilant. We threw the skis to him, he put them on, and then we threw the towrope.

"Ready? Remember, you girls are the designated spotters," Conor told Kristina and me. We positioned ourselves where we could watch Jason's every move. If he fell, or had any sort of mishap, we'd tell Conor to turn the speedboat around.

But Jason was obviously a pro. He got right up and skimmed along in our wake with no trouble at all.

"He's signaling to stop," Kristina yelled after a while. Conor slowed down and made a U-turn to pick up Jason, who was bobbing around in the waves.

"You next, Maureen," Kristina urged. "I *never* ski. I hate to get my hair wet."

I shrugged. "Okay. I'm dying to try it!"

I buckled on a life belt and jumped in while Jason was still in the water. It was wonderfully cold, like a refreshing drink that had been chilled with ice cubes.

"Here're your skis," Jason said, handing them to me. "Now, you know how to keep your heels down when you ski?"

"I think so," I said. "I watched how you did it, anyway."

"And keep your knees bent and your arms loose if you can. Elbows bent, too, okay?"

"Okay . . ." I struggled to get my feet into the rubber bindings of the skis, and finally felt secure in them. Then I had to swim a distance to reach the end of the towrope. I'm a strong swimmer, but I couldn't believe how clumsy I was in those skis!

"All set!" I called out. Jason was now back on board being a spotter with Kristina.

The powerful engine started up. My heart dropped, waiting for the tug on the rope. And then there it was, a sudden yank, and I was holding on for dear life!

The pull was fierce. All I could do was concentrate on holding on, but I was also supposed to keep my skis parallel and my knees bent and my arms loose and—

Forget it! I was down and floundering in the waves. The boat went on without me until Conor could turn around, and for a moment it was the scariest, loneliest feeling in the whole world, like being totally abandoned.

When the *Lazy Bones* came back, I felt my panic subside.

"Keep trying," Conor called out as Jason threw the towline my way again.

This time I got up for a minute or so, and then down I went, like the *Titanic*.

The third time I was more prepared for the violent tug of the rope. I made my arms bend and I got up, held on tightly, and remembered to bend my knees.

I couldn't believe I was really doing it!

I stood tall, grinning from ear to ear. I discovered that once I got the hang of it, it wasn't that hard.

When I felt really exhausted, I simply let go of the rope and sank down into the water. Conor brought the boat around, and Jason threw me a rope ladder.

"Pretty good for your first time," Jason called out.

"That was wonderful!" Kristina said sincerely.

"Not bad for a New York airhead," I heard Conor saying in his usual teasing tone, but this time I didn't take offense.

Dripping and jubilant, I climbed back into the boat and sat next to Conor. "Thanks, Conor," I said, wrapping myself in a big soft beach towel. "I really loved it!"

"You're an official water-skier now," he said solemnly. "So you get the Slimy Seaweed award."

"Uh-oh," I said. "Slimy seaweed?"

"It's a great honor," Conor insisted, draping a long ribbon of slippery green seaweed around my shoulders.

"Ugh, *gross!*" Kristina screeched.

I didn't mind at all. Conor's hands lingered on my shoulders and neck, and I was aware of how close he was to me.

"Welcome, Maureen Butler, to the great water-skiers club." Those blue eyes were studying me, and I felt a shiver down my spine.

"I'm overcome by the honor," I said in a voice that came out sort of shaky. *Strange,* I was thinking. *I handled all the scary things about waterskiing pretty well, but now I'm about to fall apart just because this boy is touching my shoulders!*

I moved away from him a couple of inches. "So who's next?" I called out loudly, trying to cover up my confusion. "Let's see *you* ski, Conor!"

The moment ended. It needed to end. I was falling under the spell of Conor Davis more and more every minute we spent together, and I didn't know what to do about it.

Chapter Six

"You're a fabulous water-skier, of course," I said to Conor when he had finished his turn. Jason piloted the boat.

"Of course," he said cheerfully as he climbed back in. He was glistening wet, and his skin looked golden in the last rays of sunlight.

"So it seems you're fabulous at everything," I said, handing him a towel.

He laughed. "*Almost* everything," he shot right back. "I just haven't learned how to be humble yet!"

After Conor had toweled himself dry, he took over the controls from Jason. "We'll head back to shore now," he said, scanning the horizon. The sun was setting, and the western sky had turned from pale blue to deep, wild pink.

As we cruised back to Kelley's Marina, I found myself thinking that I'd never had such a wonderful day in my whole life. I'd loved every minute of it. First, working on Grandpa's boat, and now this perfect evening out on the water with Conor and his friends. I'd never dreamed that I might learn to water-ski, but amazingly, I'd mastered it.

As for my feelings about Conor, I wouldn't think about them just now. I'd relax and go with the flow.

The setting sun disappeared just as we pulled into the dock space where Conor's brother kept the *Lazy Bones.* We spent the next half hour washing down the boat and making it as spotless as it was when we started out.

"I hope we do this again," Kristina said later with enthusiasm, as she climbed into Jason's car in the parking lot.

They drove off, and now Conor and I were alone in the dim, deserted parking lot of the marina. The only sound was the soft lapping of waves on the shore.

"They're such a cute couple," I said to fill the silence.

"Mmmm."

"Jason's your closest friend, I guess?"

"I guess. We've been pals since first grade."

I couldn't think of any more small talk, but it was time to get into Conor's car and start back home, anyway. Grandpa would be waiting to see that we were safe, that everything had gone all right with my first attempt at waterskiing.

So I started stuffing my gear into the car. But Conor just stood there. "Hey, Maureen . . ."

"Hey what?" I asked.

"Last night at the fireworks . . ."

"Yes?" Instantly I thought about the kiss, and I felt light-headed.

Conor said in a quiet voice, "I promised that would be the only kiss we'd ever have, remember?"

I couldn't speak, so I just nodded.

He moved closer to me and put a hand on my arm. "What if I broke that promise?"

"Oh, Conor!" I whispered.

Very gently he pulled me into his arms. We were both sticky and salty from skiing, but neither of us minded as Conor bent his head and our lips met.

It was our first real kiss, and it tasted like salt, and it was wonderful. It was so unbearably sweet that my heart began drumming.

My fortune cookie had said: Love blossoms in an unexpected place. Well, love *was* blossoming, it seemed, though I hadn't intended for this to happen.

"We hardly know each other," I murmured, still in the circle of Conor's strong arms.

"We've known each other for a long time," he contradicted. "You've been coming to Seabreeze every summer almost all our lives."

"But we weren't friends."

"No," he said, his finger tracing a line along my cheek, "but now I wish we had been."

"You said you never wanted to date a girl like me," I argued faintly.

"I know I did." He kissed me lightly on the tip of my nose. "Guess I was wrong. We have a bunch of problems to work out, don't we?"

At that, my heart soared. There had to be a way to work things out, even when two people were as different as Conor and I!

"Mmmm, you smell so good," Conor said.

I giggled. "Oh, sure! I probably smell like seaweed." Conor kissed me again. When we came up for air, I said, "Conor, my grandfather will be worrying if we don't get home soon."

"Yes." He nodded his head, but neither of us moved. We kissed softly one time more, then we reluctantly parted.

"I'm not sure what's happening here," Conor said, and I saw a little flicker of a smile cross his face. "But let's get you home and let Cap'n Andy know you didn't drown."

It was after eight o'clock when we got back to the house on Lilac Lane, but Grandpa wasn't there.

"Now what?" I wondered out loud, letting myself in with my key. Conor followed. "I wonder where he is."

Just then I found Grandpa's note:

> *Dear Maureen,*
>
> *Have gone over to watch a movie on Mrs. Mac's VCR. Call me when you get home. Come and join us if you'd like.*
>
> *Love,*
> *Grandpa.*

I turned to Conor and laughed. "Imagine that! We rushed back because we thought he'd be worried."

"Maybe he is. You should call him."

I found Mrs. Mac's number in the phone book, and I told them both about my water-skiing feats. Then Conor and I settled down on the couch in Grandpa's small, cozy living room.

"Why are we sitting so far apart?" Conor asked with a smile.

"Because—I think we need to talk," I said, trying to be reasonable and sensible, "and any more kisses would only distract us."

"Okay." Conor sat back and put his sneakered feet up on Grandpa's lobster-crate coffee table. "Let's talk."

I put my feet up, too. "You first."

The silence stretched out for what seemed a long time. Then Conor said, "I guess it's my fault all this is happening."

"Well, yes," I agreed. "You and those kisses, Conor Davis!"

"Hmmm. I wonder if what we need is more time to think?"

I felt my heart sink. "Not see each other, you mean?"

"No way!" He grinned boyishly. "We *do* need to see each other."

"I agree." I relaxed.

"We'll be together every day on the *Lucky Lindie.*"

"Yes, but we need time to be alone, too," I said. "To see where all this is heading."

He glanced at me. "You have a boyfriend back home, don't you? Cap'n Andy said something about it."

"Oh, Dennis—yes," I said. "That is, I've

been seeing him, but we're not really serious about each other."

"I was going with somebody, too, until recently."

"What happened?" I asked.

Conor sat up straighter. "Like I told you, I get really mad if anybody tries to change me. Well, Crystal started bugging me about going to college." Suddenly he scowled at me. "And I bet you'll end up doing the same thing!"

"Why should I do that?" I was indignant. "I believe each person knows what's best for himself—or herself."

"You say that now, Maureen, but I know you honor students. You don't respect anyone who doesn't have a straight-*A* average."

"That's not true!" I cried. "I have the very highest regard for people who work with their hands. Look at my grandfather! He's always been in the boating business, a master mechanic with motors. It's wonderful people like him who make the world a better place."

"That's nice, what you said about making the world a better place," he said after a while.

I looked down at my hands and smiled. "I loved what *you* said before," I murmured. "About me smelling good."

Conor smiled, too. "I meant it. You *do* smell sweet."

"I was thinking of staying here longer than two weeks," I said suddenly.

"Yeah? Great!" Conor's whole face lit up.

"Maybe the whole summer, or at least until the *Lucky Lindie* is finished. I'd like to be here for her maiden voyage. If I do stay, we'll have lots of time to get to know each other," I pointed out.

"Terrific!" Conor started to move closer to me, but right at that moment we heard Grandpa opening the front door. Immediately Conor slid back to where he had been sitting. Our magical evening was over. I couldn't help wishing for one more kiss, but it wasn't going to happen.

After some pleasant conversation with Grandpa, Conor left. As I watched him go, I marveled that I had been in Seabreeze for less than two days, and already I had fallen head over heels in love with a guy I used to hate!

Things were happening much too fast for me.

worthy than just beautifying," Conor told me one afternoon as we took a lemonade break together under a chestnut tree near the Sound. "Your grandfather's having canvas covers and seat cushions made, and he's started to buy lights, fire extinguishers, life preservers, life jackets, and other safety equipment."

"And a ship-to-shore radio," I added.

"Plus he's tuning and cleaning the motor."

"That's what Grandpa's best at," I said. "He's an absolute whiz with motors."

"Yeah. And I, of course, am entrusted with the incredibly important job of applying the anti-fouling paint to the bottom of the hull." Conor smiled smugly, pretending to be superior and triumphant.

"I'm truly impressed," I said with a straight face. "I've also seen you helping Grandpa check out the propeller shaft, rudder, bilge pump, and shaft seals." I threw all that in because I was proud to be learning all these nautical terms.

"Not bad, for a landlubber." Conor looked at me, a smile on his lips. "Not bad at all. I guess you see there's a lot more to restoring an old boat than meets the eye."

"Just like there's a lot more going on with us," I murmured.

"Yeah." He bent down and kissed me. I returned it, hoping that no one in the boat yard was watching. No one was, so we stole another. And then another.

"It seems that the guy who said we had nothing in common has changed his mind," I teased.

"Okay, we *do* have some things in common," he admitted. "I don't know if it's enough to last beyond this summer, but . . ."

"Who's looking that far ahead?" I finished for him, though secretly, I knew I was.

Conor and I were having a great time. We did something together almost every night, even if it was just taking a walk hand in hand along the water's edge or down Main Street. Sometimes on a really hot night, we'd swim out at the point until the sun set and the moon began to climb in the sky. Other nights we took out the *Lazy Bones* and water-skied with Jason and Kristina.

Once we went island-hopping, just the two of us, in the *Lazy Bones*. Those little islands out in the Sound were beautiful. Our favorite was Cliffstone Island, which was totally deserted but had once been an elegant estate. We strolled under a trellis overgrown with ancient wisteria vines, and we even found a crumbling birdbath hidden in a tangle of weeds.

"This will always be *our* island," Conor said, kissing me lightly by the birdbath.

My heart was so full of joy, I couldn't speak. It certainly sounded like he, too, wanted our relationship to continue long after summer ended.

I had never loved a boy so much before. I loved every single thing about him. I loved to hear his voice, to watch him at work on the boat, and to hear him laugh, that deep chuckle that made my heart soar to the sky.

The way I felt about Conor scared me. We were too young for this kind of intensity, especially since I had so many years of college still ahead . . .

And that was the *other* thing that scared me.

College. The more I thought about it, the more convinced I was that Conor ought to know about the Institute of Naval Architecture. It was exactly what he needed. If he went to school there and I went to Long Island University, then we'd be able to see each other all the time.

But how could I bring up the subject? I couldn't bear to take the chance of losing him.

After the second time I saw Conor's drawings, I decided I had to take that chance.

He invited me to his house on Saturday night for the weekly New England baked bean supper, with all his brothers and their wives and all of the little Davis nieces and nephews.

His mom served the meal outdoors on several picnic tables, and his father, a tall, graying man, cooked hot dogs over a rustic stone fireplace. Some of the kids danced around us, singing, "Conor's got a girlfriend . . ." but we didn't mind.

I had a great time. I was seeing Conor as the "baby" of this large family of men. He didn't behave any differently. He was still cool and confident and easygoing, but it did show me why he was so determined to follow in the footsteps of his father and brothers. They had all gone into the shipyard business and were content with their lives. Conor had probably never realized that he could use his talents to make a good life for himself doing something else.

After dinner I carried a mountain of plates into the kitchen, and Mrs. Davis thanked me profusely.

"I wanted you to see these, Maureen," she said, pulling out two more rolls of drawings. "Conor drew these last week." She waited while I unrolled them and studied them.

"They're unbelievable," I said in awe.

"I know." I could hear the pride in her voice. "His art teacher said he has a talent that's extremely rare."

"Have you ever heard of the Institute of Naval Architecture?" I asked Mrs. Davis.

"No," she said, "but it sounds like it would be the perfect school for Conor." We looked at each other for a long moment, each knowing what the other was thinking.

We were interrupted by three of her grand-daughters who wanted to help with the dishes. Mrs. Davis rolled up the drawings and patted me on the shoulder.

"Good luck, dear," she said. "Maybe you're the one who can convince him."

My plan went into action on Monday evening.

"I need to stop by the library," I told Conor. We were going window-shopping, which sim-ply meant walking up and down Main Street, peering into shop windows. It was always fun because most of the stores carried lots of nautical things.

Conor wasn't surprised. He knew how much I loved to read, and I was always taking out books.

We started to walk three blocks to the Sea-breeze Public Library. Along the way we came to Dana Harvey's Custom Boatshop, a huge workshop where Mr. Harvey, a friend of

Grandpa's, was usually hard at work on his custom-built boats.

"Oh, there's Mr. Harvey," I said, pointing. "Let's go in for a minute and say hello." I knew Conor would agree. Everyone in town knew Dana Harvey was working on a replica of an eighteenth-century sailing vessel that would eventually be transported to California and used in a Hollywood film.

What everyone *didn't* know was who had designed the sloop. But I did—Benjamin Miller. He was waiting inside for us, according to my carefully calculated plan.

"Hi, Mr. Harvey," I called out, coming up the steps and entering the cool interior of the workshop. Dana Harvey's latest creation in progress reminded me of a huge skeleton in the American Museum of Natural History. It was just a wooden spine with ribs.

"Hi, there, Maureen, Conor." Mr. Harvey was in on the plot, too. He made a few minutes of small talk, then called out, "Hey, Ben, where are you? Come out and meet two friends of mine . . ."

Mr. Miller appeared from the back of the shop. "I'd like you to meet the man who designed this sloop," Mr. Harvey said. "The esteemed naval architect, Ben Miller. Ben, this is Conor Davis and his friend Maureen."

I know it was deceitful. It was inexcusable.

But it was the only way I could think of to get Conor and Mr. Miller together, and it seemed to work like clockwork.

Conor seemed interested as he listened to all Mr. Miller had to say. Pretty soon Mr. Miller steered the conversation around to the Institute, mentioning that tuition was free for talented, deserving students.

"Conor likes to draw," I said casually. "He does terrific blueprints of ships."

"Is that so?" Both Mr. Miller and Mr. Harvey managed to look surprised and impressed.

The only one who suddenly looked grim was Conor. He must have smelled a rat, because his eyes darkened with suspicion and his jaw tightened.

"I'll mail you some literature about the Institute if you like, Conor," Mr. Miller was saying, but I had a sinking feeling we had blown it. "Would you like information about room-and-board scholarships as well?"

Conor didn't answer right away. His face was as stormy as a thundercloud. "Thank you, no. I won't be needing any of that," he finally said in a cool tone.

"Oh?" Mr. Miller said. "But I thought . . ."

"No," Conor said. "I'm really not interested." He mumbled a polite good-bye to the two men and turned on his heel. A second later he was gone, out the door and down the steps. When I caught up with him, he was already halfway up the street, passing the Historical Society.

"Conor, wait!" I called. He stopped by the big iron gate in front of the Captain Farraway House. Conor stood there glaring at me. The look on his face told me he had seen through my little scheme. His voice was angry. "That was a sneaky trick to play on me!"

"But I thought naval architecture would really interest you," I explained. "I just wanted you to . . ."

"Maureen, you deliberately set me up. That hurts me."

"I did it for your own good!" I cried. "Don't be so stubborn! You're incredibly smart and talented, but if you were just a little open-minded—"

"There's nothing more to say." I could tell he was making a great effort to remain calm. "You know the way to the library. I'm going home."

"*Why?*" I was startled and hurt. "Why, Conor? We still care for each other. Nothing can change that."

"Wrong." He reached out and yanked a fragile yellow daylily from its stem, crushing it tightly in one hand. "It's not going to work for us, Maureen," Conor said quietly. "It's obvious you're ashamed of me. You want to change me into somebody you can be proud of."

"That's not true! I only wanted—"

"You only wanted me to be someone else," he said grimly.

I was getting angry now. "I can't believe you're saying that."

"I really cared about you, Maureen. But you had to do what everyone else did." His blue eyes misted over briefly. "I won't be reconstructed by anybody, not even you. It's over, Maureen."

Then he turned and walked away.

Chapter Eleven

In every way, my beautiful golden summer had ended. It rained the next day, dark and dreary summer rain that poured in torrents and put a halt to our boat painting. According to the weather report, a severe storm was headed our way.

"Well, Connecticut needed some rain," Grandpa said philosophically. "It's been a mighty dry summer."

"It sure has," agreed Mrs. Mac. She had come over to have breakfast with us.

"So, Maureen," Grandpa said, "we have a day or two off from the boat. Have any plans?"

"No," I said around the lump in my throat.

"You and Conor don't have anything special on tap?" Mrs. Mac looked at me shrewdly, trying to figure out the expression on my face.

"Nothing," I whispered. I pushed away my bagel.

Now even Grandpa noticed that something was wrong. He and Mrs. Mac exchanged glances.

"Trouble in paradise, Maureen?" When Mrs. Mac put out a hand to touch my arm in a gentle, caring way, I was afraid I would burst into tears.

"There is no paradise," I blurted out. "Conor and I broke up last night."

Suddenly, hearing those words spoken out loud, I started to cry and I couldn't stop. Mrs. Mac folded me into her arms and hugged me. She smelled as sweet as my own grandmother used to, and it felt good to be held so tightly.

"There, there, dear," she said in a soothing tone. "You just go ahead and have that cry."

I didn't try to talk, I just sobbed for a while. Somehow it made me feel better to let it all out, even though I knew crying wasn't going to solve anything. It certainly wouldn't bring Conor back to me.

Later I explained what had happened. Grandpa felt terrible, blaming himself for putting the idea of the Naval Institute in my head in the first place. Mrs. Mac blamed Conor for being so pigheaded, and I blamed myself for meddling. But none of it helped.

All that day I went walking through the town of Seabreeze in the pouring rain, feeling lost and alone and very sad. It was hard to believe that only yesterday this town had been the happiest place on earth for me. Now my heart hurt and I felt empty. I had lost Conor. I'd done the one thing that was guaranteed to turn him off for good, and I hadn't even been honest about it. He was right. I'd played a sneaky trick on him, and he would never trust me again.

For two whole days I took long walks in the rain. I couldn't even lose myself in my beloved novels. As I walked, I tried to figure out what to do.

Should I go back home? I seriously considered it, and then vetoed that idea. No, I was determined to see the completion of the *Lucky Lindie.* I had worked hard on her, and besides, I knew how much Grandpa loved having me around, especially since he was so busy. I was able to make life easier for him by doing the laundry, helping him cook, and tidying up the kitchen after our meals.

No, I wouldn't run away. Even if Conor

didn't care about me any longer, I wasn't a bad person. I had to try to hang on to my self-esteem, no matter how hard it was to do.

On the third day it was still raining, but Grandpa and I still did everything we could for the *Lindie* in spite of the weather. We went shopping at boat stores up and down the coast, purchasing many items the boat would need. We also picked up the new canvas covers Grandpa had ordered that would snap around the boat for protection after each outing.

As busy as we were, I couldn't chase away the gloom inside me. I missed Conor terribly. If only I could see him, talk to him, or at least try to salvage our friendship. But I didn't know how to make the first move, so I hung around with Grandpa, marking time until the rain stopped.

On Saturday morning, my mother called.

"Maureen, I think you should know that Uncle Reggie is planning a visit to Seabreeze next week," she said. "He wanted it to be a surprise, but I thought you should prepare Grandpa."

"Oh, great, Mom," I said gloomily. "Just what we need! He's always such a barrel of fun."

"He's coming for a reason, dear. He's really

serious about getting Grandpa to move near us."

"Grandpa doesn't want to move to some horrible retirement home in New York," I argued. "You know that, Mom. How can you side with Uncle Reggie?"

"I don't, Maureen." She hesitated for a moment. "Well, perhaps in a way I do. I would like my father living nearby, so we could take care of him."

"He doesn't need taking care of. Trust me. He's got a wonderful life here, Mom. There's even a neighbor who cooks and sews and cleans for him."

"A neighbor? Who?"

"A really nice woman named Claire Mac-Phearson. She's a widow. I call her Mrs. Mac."

"A *woman*?" My mother sounded slightly shocked. Mom likes to think she's thoroughly modern, liberated, and up-to-date about everything, but the idea of her widowed father having a girlfriend was just too much for her, I could tell.

"Then I'm really glad Reggie is going out there for a visit," Mom said. "We need to know the whole story."

"*What* whole story?"

"The whole story about this woman, and

about Grandpa's health. What he can do and what he can't do . . ."

"Okay, Mom. I'll tell Grandpa that Uncle Reggie's coming," I sighed.

"You're still staying there all summer, Maureen?"

"I don't know. Maybe I'll be home in August," I said, thinking that by then our work on the boat would be done.

"Oh, Dennis will be glad to hear that. Why don't you give him a call?"

I hadn't even thought about Dennis in a long time. I'd been so wrapped up in Conor, and then my misery about losing Conor . . . "I'll call him," I said without much interest. "Maybe."

I would never have told Grandpa that Uncle Reggie was definitely coming if I'd known how upset he would get.

"This is terrible," he said, wringing his hands. "Didn't your mother say what *day* he's coming? What if he tracks us down at the boat yard? What if he carries on the way he always does? I don't want to listen to his tirades—"

"Calm down, Grandpa, *please*," I begged. "He won't find out about the boat. We'll go over our Reggie Drill again, okay?"

But Grandpa didn't calm down. He grew

more and more agitated all day Saturday. By evening I could tell there was something physically wrong with him. When he thought I wasn't looking, he'd rub his chest as if it hurt. He also seemed to be having trouble breathing.

I wished Mrs. Mac was there to talk to, but she'd gone to Rhode Island for a couple of days to visit her daughter.

"Maybe we should call Dr. Barnett," I suggested. "Just to tell him you're not feeling one hundred percent."

"Nonsense," Grandpa said grumpily. "There's no reason to bother him. I'll be fine."

But as the hours passed, Grandpa was not fine, I could tell. He didn't eat any supper and once I saw him taking one of his nitro-glycerin pills. After that, for a little while, he was breathing better. As we sat quietly in the living room, I pretended to be interested in the TV shows, but I was really watching him closely.

At eleven o'clock that night Grandpa fell asleep in his old easy chair, but he kept clutching his chest even in his sleep, and he was moaning. I was terrified. I didn't know what to do, but I knew I had to do something.

"Grandpa, wake up," I said, shaking him gently. "Wake up! I'm going to take you down to the hospital."

His eyes flew open. "No, Maureen!" He looked angry, and I'd never known him to be angry with me before. "I won't go! That's all Reggie needs to hear, then he'd have a real case."

"Grandpa, I'm getting crazy with worry!"

"Well, you can stop worrying," he snapped. "Everybody worries about me too much. Go talk a walk or something and let me sleep."

A *walk*? Was he suggesting that I take a walk, alone, at eleven PM? Now I knew something was wrong.

"Maybe I *will* take a walk," I said, to see if he'd change his mind. But he just grunted and dozed off, snoring almost immediately.

Desperate now, I decided I had to call Dr. Barnett. But when I picked up the receiver, there was no dial tone. The storm had apparently knocked out the phone lines. There was only one place I could go for help—Conor's house. I was sure that either he or his parents would be able to get Grandpa to the hospital, whether he wanted to go or not. I just hoped I wasn't going to wake them.

I put on my waterproof poncho and ran out the door, sloshing through puddles and ignoring the rain that continued to pour down. To my relief, I saw lights in the Davises' windows. I must have looked like a drowned rat by the time I knocked on the door.

Conor opened it. When he saw me, he stared. "Maureen?"

"Yes, it's me. Conor, I need help. It's Grandpa—he's—"

Conor didn't let me finish. Without even bothering to grab an umbrella, he shot out the door, and together we raced to Grandpa's house.

"Captain Andy," Conor said softly when we went into the living room, "what's the matter? You're not feeling well?"

"I'm fine!" Grandpa sounded even grumpier at being awakened again. "Maureen is simply being a hysterical female. Like her mother!" But both Conor and I could see that he had a strangely gray pallor.

"I don't think you *are* fine, sir," Conor said firmly. "At any rate, we're going to get you checked out. Now where's your raincoat? We're taking a ride down to the hospital ER."

"That's ridiculous," Grandpa grumbled, but thankfully, this time he didn't refuse.

I gave Conor the truck keys, and he went out to start the motor while I dug out a raincoat for Grandpa and found his old galoshes.

But Conor came rushing back into the house a moment later looking frantic.

"Something's wrong with the truck, Maureen." He ran his fingers through his wet hair. "I can't get it to move!"

"It's probably the shifting linkage again," I said. I remembered when Grandpa had showed me how to fix it, but did I still know how? That had been weeks ago; I'd never driven the truck all that time.

"You know what to do?" Conor asked. He glanced over at Grandpa, who was looking more and more gray every minute. We didn't have a lot of time to waste.

"I'll try," I said. "You bring Grandpa out."

So in the pouring rain, and the pitch black, I practically climbed under the hood. I was too short to reach in easily, so I had to hoist myself up onto the body of the truck. Then I had to unjam the shifting linkage. It took me several tries, but finally I did it.

I couldn't help feeling kind of proud of myself by the time I climbed into the cab next to Grandpa.

As Conor started the engine, he glanced over at me. "Not bad at all, for an airhead New York girl," he said.

I'd have enjoyed that backhanded praise under any other circumstances. But as it was, we were hurtling through the night toward Seabreeze Hospital, the rain pouring down the truck windows in sheets, and Grandpa was definitely not in good shape.

Chapter Twelve

"Help! This man is having chest pains," Conor called out as we piloted Grandpa through the sliding glass doors of the Emergency Room.

A couple of attendants immediately took Grandpa away. They could see how gray he looked and all pinched around the mouth. He was obviously in pain.

Conor and I were left to answer some questions and fill out forms at the reception desk. It wasn't long before I heard a nurse paging Dr. Barnett.

"I hope it isn't too late," I whispered, grasping Conor's wrist. "But honestly, Grandpa wouldn't let me get help sooner—"

"Don't torture yourself, Maureen." Conor spoke softly and put a comforting arm around me. "You did just fine." He led me over to a waiting room full of chairs and couches, sat me down, and held my hand tightly.

"When will they let us know?" I wondered aloud, then jumped up to ask the nurse at the desk what she could tell me.

"We think your grandfather is going to be just fine," she said. "Dr. Barnett is with him right now."

In no time at all, Dr. Barnett came out of Grandpa's cubicle with a reassuring smile for Conor and me.

"Don't worry, kids," he said. "Cap'n Andy is going to be all right. You did the right thing in bringing him here."

"But what happened?" I asked. "Was it a heart attack?"

"No," Dr. B. answered. "He was so upset about your uncle coming that he got himself all worked up. That caused the angina, which only means chest pain. But his pacemaker is in perfect shape, and so's he."

Tears of relief started rolling down my cheeks. "Are you sure, Dr. Barnett?" I asked.

"Positive, Maureen. I'm doing a number of tests on your grandfather, but I know him pretty well. When he's under a lot of stress, his chest muscles go into spasm. It's *not* a heart attack."

"Can he go home tonight, then?" Conor asked.

The doctor clicked his tongue regretfully. "I have to keep all angina patients here for three days, just to be on the safe side. But please don't think that means there's a problem."

Three days!

"Dr. B.," I said, "I have to tell my mother. I can't keep something like this from her."

Dr. Barnett nodded. "Of course not, Maureen. Would it help if I called her for you?"

"Yes!" I blurted out. I knew Mom would believe the doctor when he said Grandpa was going to be okay, but if I called, she'd jump in the car and drive to Seabreeze immediately.

"Fine. I'll call her first thing in the morning. If I phone at this hour, she'll be sure Andy is at death's door," Dr. Barnett said. "Now Maureen, do you have a place to go tonight so you won't be all alone?"

"She can stay with us, Dr. B.," Conor said quickly. "My folks will be glad to have her. We have a lot of empty bedrooms."

I looked at him in surprise and gratitude. Then I gave Dr. Barnett my home phone number, and he went to check on his other patients while Conor and I visited with Grandpa for a few minutes.

Grandpa looked small and pale against the mound of white pillows that propped him up, but he smiled when he saw us, and that's when I knew he was going to be fine.

"They're keeping me here for a while," Grandpa grumbled. "I guess I have to obey my doctor, but there goes my schedule for finishing the boat."

"Don't worry about the *Lindie* now," Conor said. "Just concentrate on getting well."

"We ought to leave you here all week, Grandpa," I scolded. "You gave us a terrible scare, being so stubborn."

"I know." He squeezed my hand. "I'm sorry, Maureen."

I kissed him on his forehead. "I guess I can forgive you," I said, choked up. "You just hurry up and get well!"

By the time we left the hospital, the rain had stopped. Conor drove the truck back to Lilac Lane without saying much. "Want to take a walk?" he asked after he parked in front of Grandpa's house.

"Now?" I asked, startled. "It's almost one in the morning."

"You'll be safe," Conor assured me. "I need

to talk to you, Maureen." He took my hand and helped me out of the truck.

We walked along Shore Road. The occasional streetlamp threw thin, misty rays of illumination along our path, so the world was mostly dark and mysterious. A few houses, though, still had lights in the windows.

"Thank you for helping with Grandpa tonight," I said simply. "I'd never have made it without you."

"I think you would have done just fine," Conor said.

"No." I shook my head. "Without you, he would never have agreed to go to the hospital."

"I'm just glad I could help you."

We walked along in silence for a while. At last Conor said, "Maureen . . ." He was having trouble beginning. "Maureen, when something like this happens—"

"Yes?"

He looked down at me. "Doesn't it make you realize how short life can be?"

I nodded. "Yes, of course . . ."

"What I mean is, it makes you realize what a short time we have to be with people we care about."

I felt a shiver run down my spine.

"What I *really* mean—" Conor stopped walking and stood next to me under a spreading elm tree. His face looked strained. I'd never seen him at a loss for words before.

"Yes?" I prompted. "What you really mean is—?"

"Maureen, I really care for you. A lot." He had finally gotten the words out, and my heart began to hammer in my chest.

"I feel the same way," I whispered, "but—"

"But what? Is it too late for us?"

"Conor, *you* were the one who broke it off," I reminded him sadly. "Or have you forgotten?"

"No, I haven't. I couldn't." He put a tentative hand on my shoulder. "Can we put that all behind us and start over, maybe?"

There was nothing I wanted more, but I had to be very clear about this. "I was the one who tricked you into meeting Mr. Miller, remember?"

"I know, and I acted like a real jerk. I actually loved meeting him and hearing about that school."

"I knew it!" I cried with joy. "So you're not angry anymore?"

He grinned. "Angry? I'm trying to apologize here!" Then his smile faded. "I'm sorry I let my stubborn pride get in the way. You were just trying to show me that I have other options."

"I was," I said. "But I guess I could have done it differently. More honestly."

He touched my cheek very gently. "I think we're both trying to apologize," he said. "And now that we have, the bottom line is that I love you, Maureen Butler."

I took a deep breath, trying to calm the rapid beating of my heart. "That's an incredible bottom line," I whispered. "I love you, too. No matter what, I love you, Conor Davis!"

We must have walked for another hour through the streets of Seabreeze, talking and kissing and smoothing things out between us. When we finally got back to Conor's house, his parents were waiting up for us. Mrs. Davis had already checked with the hospital and knew that Grandpa was resting comfortably.

"Well, look at you two," she said with a grin when we walked in, our arms around each other. "Together again!"

After she had set me up in one of the empty bedrooms upstairs, I tossed and turned for a while, my mind in a whirl. Grandpa was going to be all right, and Conor had said he loved me! What a night this had been! I was so happy that I even forgot to worry about Uncle Reggie's impending visit.

Chapter Thirteen

Three days later, when Grandpa was to be released from the hospital, the *Lucky Lindie* was ready to be launched. But Grandpa didn't know it. Dr. Barnett and I had agreed not to tell him about our labors.

Still keeping the secret, I drove the truck to the hospital to pick Grandpa up. He wanted to go straight to Kelley's Marina.

"I'd just like to look at the boat," Grandpa said wistfully. "We won't work on her until tomorrow, but just let me have a little look."

"Sure," I agreed cheerfully. "Why not?"

We pulled into Kelley's. When we reached the spot where the *Lindie* had been, there was nothing but an empty scaffold.

Grandpa turned pale. "Where's my boat? Where's the *Lucky Lindie*?"

"Now calm down and don't have another angina attack," a voice said. It was Dr. Barnett, who leaned in through the truck window to smile at Grandpa.

"But—where's my boat?" Grandpa asked again.

"Look," I told him, pointing out toward the water. "There she is!"

We got out of the truck and hurried over. The *Lindie* was hoisted up into the air in a sling, which was attached to a crane that moved boats around. She hung suspended there, glittering like the most perfect jewel of the sea.

I watched Grandpa's brown eyes fill with happy tears. "Now I see what you did," he whispered. "You finished her while I was in the hospital!"

"Sure. She's completely restored and ship-shape." Conor walked over and put his arm around my grandfather. "We hope we did everything right."

"Incredible!" Grandpa's face was shining with joy. "She's absolutely perfect." He turned to face Conor. "You knew exactly how I wanted her to be, and there she is!"

"So you approve, Captain? Then she's ready to be launched!"

Mr. Kelley came out of his office carrying an enormous bottle of champagne. Bea was with him, and so were Jason, Kristina, and Mrs. Mac. "Who's going to christen her, Captain Andy?" asked Mr. Kelley.

"How about Mrs. Mac?" suggested Bea.

"No, no," Mrs. Mac protested. "This job should be done by only one person—the granddaughter of Linda Claiborne."

Everyone cheered. Grandpa gave me a thumbs-up sign, and Mr. Kelley handed me the champagne bottle.

I was stunned. This was an honor I'd never expected.

"How do you do it?" I asked, and Conor stepped in to show me.

"Just slam the bottle against the hull of the boat." He pointed. "Right there—*whack*."

"Oh, no," I groaned, "and ruin our beautiful paint job?"

Everyone laughed.

I had something vital to tell them before I broke the bottle. I cleared my throat and said, "My grandmother Linda knew that Grandpa had an important dream," I announced. "She realized he wanted to restore a wonderful old wooden boat. And sure enough, as of today, he's done it!"

There was wild applause, not only from our little group but also from other boat owners and workers in the boat yard. "I had a lot of help from a lot of good people," Grandpa said, overcome with emotion.

Now it was time. I raised the champagne bottle.

"I christen thee . . . the *Lucky Lindie!*" I yelled dramatically, then swung the bottle hard against the boat. As it shattered, there was another big round of applause.

Then everybody on the *Lindie* crew started hugging, kissing, and congratulating everyone around.

"Time to put her in the water," commanded Mr. Kelley, waving his arm at the man who was operating the launching crane.

I watched, spellbound, as the huge apparatus swung the cabin cruiser up and across toward the water.

"It's a great sight, isn't it?" Conor asked, standing behind me with both hands on my shoulders.

"Unbelievable," I said. I felt so happy, I almost thought I would burst.

We all held our breath, then cheered in unison when the *Lindie* touched down on the gentle surface of the harbor. Mr. Kelley climbed aboard, checked the bilge, and secured the boat to the dock.

"She'll begin to spring leaks," Conor told me. "But don't worry—a few days in the water and her planks will swell up again. The bilge pumps will be working all the time to empty out the excess water."

Now it was party time. Mr. Kelley and Bea had set up picnic tables outside his office for the big celebration.

What a party it was! Balloons, taped music, and delicious food cooked by Mrs. Mac, Bea, Mrs. Davis, Mrs. Barnett, and me. Grandpa still had to take it easy, but he was so happy! We all were. We enjoyed the day thoroughly, and all we could think of was the *Lucky Lindie*'s maiden voyage, the first cruise we'd take when the boat was ready to go.

For the next couple of days we went to the boat yard, boarded the *Lucky Lindie*, and checked on her progress, and each day we found less and less water seeping in between the dry old planks. By the fourth day, there was almost no seawater at all coming in or being pumped out.

"I think we're there," Grandpa said, and Mr. Kelley and Conor agreed. "It's time to take our first cruise," Grandpa continued. "Got to see how that engine works."

Conor, Grandpa, and I went home that afternoon feeling excited about the *Lindie*'s maiden voyage, which would take place tomorrow morning. We were even singing some old sea shanties as we drove along Shore Road.

But our happiness was short-lived. There, sitting on the front step of the Lilac Lane house, was trouble, in the form of a fiercely scowling Uncle Reggie!

"Remember, not one word about the boat," whispered Grandpa.

"Of course not." I put a hand on my grandfather's arm. "He has no way of finding out. Relax."

"Yeah," Conor said. "Everything's going to be okay. Don't you dare get stressed again!"

We got out of the truck and faced Uncle Reggie, who stood up, his red hair glinting in the late-afternoon sun. He looked as though he'd forgotten how to smile.

"Where have you been, Dad?" he demanded without even saying hello. "I went to the hospital first, but they said you'd been released days ago. Then I came here, to find the door unlocked and nobody home. What if a burglar had come in? What if . . ."

"Hello, Reggie," Grandpa said calmly.

"*Hello?* Is that all you can say when you've scared me half to death?" Uncle Reggie bellowed.

"I think you'd better let Grandpa go inside," I said quickly. "He's a little tired. Just out of the hospital, you know . . ."

"You should have thought of that before you took him gallivanting!" Uncle Reggie moved aside, however, and let Grandpa go indoors, where he sat down on the old sofa.

"We weren't gallivanting, Uncle Reggie . . ." I began.

"No," my uncle retorted, "I imagine you went over to that boat you've been working on!"

Conor, Grandpa, and I stared at him in absolute silence. How could he have known?

Uncle Reggie held up the small notebook that Grandpa had been writing in all summer. He must have left it on one of the tables in the living room.

"Forgot about this, didn't you?" Uncle Reggie waved the notebook under Grandpa's nose. "Well, it's all in here, everything you've been doing!"

"Uncle Reggie," I protested, "please don't—"

"Keep quiet, Maureen. Now I know why my father landed in the hospital! You've allowed him to overexert himself."

"That's not true, sir," Conor said hotly. "We've done all the strenuous stuff. The captain only had to direct us."

"The captain!" Uncle Reggie repeated angrily. "Don't make me laugh. My father is a sick old man, not a captain."

"You're absolutely wrong," I said bravely to my uncle. "Grandpa's *not* sick, and he knows more about restoring boats than anyone in Connecticut—maybe anywhere!"

"Don't you see what this restoration has done to him?" Uncle Reggie glared at me. "It landed him in the hospital! Do you think I want to lose my father three years after I lost my mother?"

"No," I said with tears springing to my eyes. "Of course not. But—"

"We won't discuss it right now," Grandpa suddenly broke in, his voice firm and steady. "Let's drop it, Reggie, for the time being."

With great effort, Uncle Reggie controlled himself. "Fine. We can talk about this in the morning. In the meantime, I'll be doing some checking up on you, Dad. And if you think you're actually going to risk your health further by sailing that boat, you have another thing coming!"

As Uncle Reggie stalked purposefully out of the house, I sat down beside Grandpa. I was worried about him. What if he had another angina attack?

But oddly enough, he didn't look upset. "I'll be fine," Grandpa told me, patting my hand. A slight smile lit up his round face. "Don't worry—I still have a few tricks up my sleeve."

I didn't know what Grandpa meant by "tricks up my sleeve," and he refused to tell me. But very early the next morning, I found out.

"Wake up, Maureen," Grandpa whispered, shaking me as I slept. "Rise and shine!"

"What—?" I mumbled, alarmed. "Whatizzit?"

"Shhh." He put a finger to his lips. "Hurry up and get dressed. We have a boat trip to take!" And he tiptoed out of my room.

Astonished, I leapt out of bed. I dressed in boating clothes, a bathing suit under jeans and a sweatshirt, and my deck shoes. Then I tiptoed down the stairs, too, so Uncle Reggie, who was sleeping in the other guest room, wouldn't hear me.

Grandpa was waiting outside by his truck. It was still dark outside. I climbed into the truck beside him, and we drove quickly to Kelley's Marina. "The boat's all ready to go," Grandpa said with determination, "and so am I. I'm not going to be cheated out of this voyage!"

Waiting for us on the dock were Mrs. Mac, Dr. Barnett, and Conor, all bundled up for the chilly early-morning air. We grinned like mischievous children who are about to outsmart their kindergarten teacher.

Just as the first pink light of dawn began to touch the eastern clouds, we rowed out to where the *Lindie* was moored and climbed aboard. Grandpa started up the engine for

129

its first time in the water, and it purred like a cat.

"Ahoy, mates! Over the bounding main we go!" Dr. Barnett shouted, making us all laugh.

Grandpa took his place at the helm, looking like an official captain. He grinned from ear to ear when Conor put a real captain's hat on Grandpa's bald head and saluted him. We were on our way!

The *Lindie* chugged out of the harbor, toward the Sound. Gulls squawked overhead against a backdrop of clouds that appeared luminescent in pink and gold.

It was a glorious morning. At first we had the harbor all to ourselves, but soon we began to see fishing boats as well as other pleasure craft. Everywhere, people turned to stare at the magnificent old Chris-Craft, and then they'd wave, as if appreciating a job well-done. We were all having the time of our lives, especially Grandpa. Best of all, we had fooled Uncle Reggie. We had gotten away from him, and he couldn't holler at us until the *Lindie*'s maiden voyage had been completed.

"By then," Grandpa told me gleefully, "it won't matter what Reggie has to say. At least we'll have had one fabulous day."

Chapter Fourteen

Whenever I think of that trip, I remember it as being absolutely perfect. As the *Lindie* chugged across the Sound to Long Island, the wind was in our faces and Uncle Reggie was behind us. Among all the pleasure craft we passed, there was just one rich, dark classic made of wood—the *Lucky Lindie*.

"This boat sure is a charmer," Dr. Barnett said at noon, as we anchored and prepared for a picnic lunch on the deck.

"She's a wonderful boat," Mrs. Mac agreed, passing out sandwiches and lemonade. "You did a marvelous job, Andrew."

"We love you, Grandpa," I said, raising my glass of lemonade in a toast. "You turned a pitiful old wreck into this fantastic cabin cruiser."

"And that's not all," Conor said, winking at me. "Captain Andy even turned this pitiful New York landlubber into a pretty able deckhand."

I playfully punched him. Then my friends gave me a round of applause, and I know I turned beet-red. But I felt terrific. I wasn't just studious Maureen who always had her nose in a book and who got all A's. I wasn't hopeless with anything resembling physical labor anymore. As Conor had said, I was a pretty able deckhand!

After lunch, some of us decided to take a swim, and when we had dried off on deck, the *Lucky Lindie* continued on her way to Long Island.

I'd had no idea that the Institute of Naval Architecture was right on the Sound, or that Grandpa was heading the boat in that direction, but he was. As we neared the school, he came as close to shore as possible so we could take a look at the campus.

"There it is," Conor said. "That's the school I'm going to apply to."

"Oh, Conor, it looks wonderful. I think it's great that you made this decision." I gazed at the big old brick buildings surrounded by all trees, and at the many boats that were ocked alongside the waterfront.

Conor shook his head in a worried way. I'm not quite sure what I'm getting myself nto, but SATs, here I come!"

"You'll knock 'em dead, Conor," Dr. Barnett said, clapping him on the back.

"Thanks, Dr. B.," Conor said quietly. Then he put his arm around me and gave me a hug. "And thank *you*, Maureen," he whispered into my ear.

It was around six o'clock when the *Lucky Lindie* chugged back into Seabreeze Harbor, heading for Kelley's Marina. We'd been out since before dawn, and we were ready to come home. Still, the closer we got to shore, the more our feelings of apprehension increased.

When we made the turn around Cullighan's Neck, a piece of land that jutted out into the harbor, we saw to our dismay that Uncle Reggie was standing on the dock at the marina. And he wasn't alone.

"Oh, my gosh, look at that!" Grandpa said, his eyebrows shooting up. I half hoped he'd turn the *Lindie* around and head for the Sound again, but of course he didn't.

"Who *is* that?" I asked peering to see who was with my uncle. "Looks like a couple of doctors. Those two men are carrying medical bags!"

"Is he going to put you away in a hospital somewhere?" asked Mrs. Mac with great alarm. "If he is, I'll have something to say about that!"

"Now, now, don't get all excited," Grandpa said. "Reggie doesn't have any real power over me."

But I still felt a rush of fear as the boat got closer to the docks. What was Uncle Reggie planning?

When we drew in even closer, I saw two other people I hadn't noticed before—my mother and father! Now I was *really* worried. Would this be doomsday for both Grandpa and me?

The minute Grandpa eased the *Lindie* into a slip and turned off the motor, Uncle Reggie started yelling.

"What's the matter with you, Dad? Sailing off like that before we even had a chance to talk! You have no idea what you've put me through!"

"Well, Reginald," Grandpa said calmly, "you have no idea what you've put *me* through, either."

"That's right." Dr. Barnett stepped in to defend Grandpa. "I'm Andy's physician, Mr. Claiborne, and if it hadn't been for all your badgering, he wouldn't have had that angina attack in the first place."

"That's ridiculous," Uncle Reggie blustered. "Now *these* two doctors are eminent cardiologists from Manhattan. I paid them a great deal of money to come here and examine my father."

"Hi there, Dave," Dr. Barnett said to one of the doctors. To the other, he said, "Hi, Jake."

"You know each other?" Uncle Reggie looked astounded.

"Of course. All of us 'eminent' cardiologists know each other." Dr. B. winked at me.

Uncle Reggie glared at Dr. B. "If you're my father's doctor, what are you doing on this boat?"

"Having fun," Dr. Barnett said. "And I can assure you that your father is in excellent health. Working on this boat all summer has been the best thing in the world for him!"

Just then my parents, who had been hovering in the background, came forward. "Maureen, hello! And Dad . . ." My mother was staring at the polished wood of the *Lindie*. "This boat is absolutely beautiful!"

"It certainly is," my father said with genuine respect in his voice. He reached out and ran a hand across the satiny wood of the hull. "What an amazing restoration."

135

"Thank you, Tom," Grandpa said with quiet dignity.

Uncle Reggie's face turned bright red. "Will all of you stop that! You're missing the point here!" He turned to Mom. "Our father has been destroying his health doing who knows what—"

"Your father," the cardiologist named Dave interrupted, "is evidently in very good hands. Dr. Barnett is one of the best men in the field."

Uncle Reggie didn't want to hear that. He looked around for someone to side with him.

"Your father has been having the time of his life this summer. From the looks of him, he could probably restore ten more boats if he feels like it," Jake, the other cardiologist, added.

"Oh, this is ridiculous!" For a lawyer, Uncle Reggie seemed to be running out of arguments. "Julie!" He turned to my mother again. "You're my sister. Tell them that Dad belongs in New York, in a retirement home near us."

My mother was silent for a moment. All eyes were on her, and I held my breath. "Reggie, I'm afraid you're on the wrong track," she finally said, smiling.

"Julie, for heaven's sake!" my uncle groaned.

"As a matter of fact, you're *wrong*," my

mother said. "Dad looks better than he has
in years, and his doctor is obviously excellent."

"Just look at this unbelievable boat they've
created," my father added.

At that, Uncle Reggie must have finally realized he was defeated. He'd counted on the
doctors and my parents to back him up, but
they were all on Grandpa's side. His face was
so red that I began to wonder if *he* was going
to have an angina attack.

"I never—" Uncle Reggie sputtered. He
seemed to be struggling for words. "I didn't
mean to cause any trouble. I just wanted—"

"You wanted what was best for Dad," my
mother finished for him, and put a hand on
Uncle Reggie's shoulder. "We all do. And now
that we've seen the evidence—this boat, and
all his friends—we can see that the best thing
for Dad is to stay right here in Seabreeze."

Sighing with relief, I went over to Conor,
who was checking the lines in the stern so
the *Lindie* would be secure. He looked up as
I approached, and our eyes met. I smiled at
him, wanting to tell him that he was the best
thing that had ever happened to me.

I couldn't wait for my parents to meet
him, and I imagined that Grandpa probably
wanted them to meet Mrs. Mac, too. There
was so much to tell now that all our secrets
were tumbling out of the closet!

My grandmother Linda had been right, I thought. Dreams can become goals, and goals can become realities. Grandpa's *wooden ship dream* had turned into a reality, and even Conor had traded his stubborn old ideas for new dreams and goals. As for me, Conor had made my dream of romance come true. I loved Conor Davis, and he loved me. We'd shared a fantastic, productive summer, and with any luck, it looked like we had prospects for a bright future, too.